Jean-Christophe Valtat

Translated from the French by Mitzi Angel

Farrar, Straus and Giroux / New York

Farrar, Straus and Giroux
18 West 18th Street, New York 10011

Copyright © 2005 by Éditions Gallimard
Translation copyright © 2010 by Mitzi Angel
Distributed in Canada by D&M Publishers, Inc.
Printed in the United States of America
Originally published in 2005 by Éditions Gallimard, France
Published in the United States by Farrar, Straus and Giroux
First American edition, 2010

Library of Congress Cataloging-in-Publication Data
Valtat, Jean-Christophe, 1968–
    [03. English]
    03 / Jean-Christophe Valtat ; [translated from the French by Mitzi
Angel]. — 1st American ed.
        p.   cm.
    ISBN: 978-0-374-10021-6 (pbk. : alk. paper)
    1. Teenage boys—Fiction.   2. Teenage girls—Fiction.   3. Teenagers
with disabilities—Fiction.   4. Adolescence—Fiction.   I. Angel, Mitzi.
II. Title.   III. Title: Zero 3.   IV. Title: Zero three.

PQ2682.A438O1813 2010
844'.92—dc22

                                                    2010012616

Designed by Jonathan D. Lippincott

www.fsgbooks.com

1   3   5   7   9   10   8   6   4   2

This work, published as part of a program providing publication assistance,
received financial support from the French Ministry of Foreign Affairs, the
Cultural Services of the French Embassy in the United States, and FACE
(French American Cultural Exchange).

*Cet ouvrage a bénéficié du soutien des Programmes d'aide à la publication de
Culturesfrance/Ministére français des affaires éstrangères et europèennes.* (This work,
published as part of a program of aid for publication, received support from
CulturesFrance and the French Ministry of Foreign Affairs.)

From the bus stop across the street it was hard to tell, but suddenly I understood, seeing the passengers in the van that collected her every morning, that she was slightly retarded. Once you knew, it was easy to make sense of her thin adolescent frame, her black hair spiking up on her little head as though she were enduring some slow, endless horror, her eyes, like those of a heroine in a Japanese cartoon forced open onto the real world, eyes so round and so opaque that if they'd focused on me, I might almost have picked them up like two black marbles rolling in the gutter at my feet. It was harder to guess her age; imagine someone whose growth had suddenly stopped, useless and discouraged or, seeing that it had dwarfed the rest of her, had chosen to freeze her body at a jarring, already awkward fourteen years of age. And yet, at first glance, I had found her pretty; her fragility moved me, or rather, I found it touching that she was so pretty, even as I worried that this pale, poorly articulated delicacy would almost certainly fall victim to the filthy urges of abusive teachers or the fumbling and hasty advances of other disabled children. I was sad that this beauty would never be truly seen by those around her or that, even if they did see it, it could never be communicated to her or that, even if it was, it would never make sense to her. But even as I formed this thought, my sadness had already turned into a kind of desire, a vague excitement I could feel in my gut, not unlike the jitters one feels on the diving platform at the pool, as though I was drawn to her precisely for the chance to love a beauty that had no self-awareness and of which, consequently, I alone would be the sole and watchful guardian. Or maybe I was jealous (for what I felt toward her was, actually, from the very start, a form of jealousy), not because she might be subjected to sexual desires beyond my grasp, but because in that unknown world—those white buildings on the hill where the bus took her—someone else, however retarded, might also find her beautiful and love her and, I didn't know why exactly, that idea seemed, in its very generosity, more repellent than all the rest, as though it stripped me of the privileges I enjoyed thanks to my normal intelligence. How to approach her (because that was question number one) I had no idea. I couldn't possibly cross the street in the dawn light and speak to her directly: first because I felt held as though on a leash by my bus stop and wouldn't dream of missing the public transport meant to hand me over to school; more to the point, because her mother (whose face, strangely, held so little interest for me that I couldn't have recognized her from one sighting to the next) rarely let go of her hand, or allowed her daughter to let go of her own, until it was time to board the bus. All the same, since her mother walked her there every morning, I imagined they must not live too far from the bus stop, so logically all I had to do was wait for her return and follow them home and sooner or later put myself in their path. This was easier said than done because I hadn't the slightest idea when a person might come back from a place like the one she went to, and if I did know the time, who was to say I'd be available, free to do as I pleased. Locked in her state of unteachable ignorance, it occurred to me, she might be kept away for something like an entire workday, until it was too late for me, with the limited movements of a twelfth grader, to meet her like a lover running off to a tryst: I had certainly never seen her on her way home, which was hardly a surprise because while I could wait to board the bus in the morning, my return offered no such opportunity. Suppose her schedule was more or less like a regular student's schedule (after all, disturbing as it was to think so, there were ineluctable similarities between her predicament and my own, beginning with our shared morning routine and the rituals of transportation), I would then have had to wait who knows how long from the moment I got off my bus until she returned, and this might happen any time as late as seven o'clock, far too late for me to explain, because I was, like her, an overprotected schoolchild in a town where nothing at all could plausibly have distracted me from my records and books for any length of time. Besides, even if I'd come up with some far-fetched excuses for my delay (since one evening was all I needed to figure out when she got home), I would still, during this unlikely wait for a bus I had no intention of boarding, have to pretend that I wanted to do just that, all the while standing there exposed to unwelcome stares on the pinkish gravel of the sidewalk, standard issue in this hostile suburb, with its looping roundabouts, its homes with façades that grazed the eye like gravel against the knee, bristling with spiny shrubbery and often guarded by a "dangerous dog" I took bitter pleasure in spitting on through the wrought-iron bars of the gate. Maybe I could have asked the institution when exactly she was sent home, but quite apart from my being too shy to face any such undertaking, with all its foreseeable complications, I didn't know which of these places to ask; the center on the hillside that I've already mentioned had simply popped into my head, without my bothering to question it, and for reasons that had nothing to do with plausibility. I'd leaped to embrace the idea thanks to the name of the institution—Rocher Fleuri, "flowering rock"—and, more precisely, for the grip it held over the local imagination and, even more locally, over the imagination I called my own.

Schoolchildren, and later middle schoolers, often used the name, although less frequently over the years, when trading insults—sometimes to tell their friends where they really came from, or else to say where they were going to end up. And I'd lost count of the times I'd heard my parents mention it when, driving behind a wheezing bus, we watched unruly mongoloids mimic us and make faces from the safety of the backseat. Whatever its literary merits, the poetic force of the name provided much of its appeal and gave me easy food for thought. On the one hand, it demonstrated, according to a tacit law almost universally observed, a sort of national principle by which the more pastoral a place-name sounded, the more safely you could assume that the official Arcadia hid the empty eye sockets of blight: moldering housing projects, schools for dunces in highly inflammable prefabs with roofs that would fly off the moment a storm broke (this happened at my school, a rare instance of the sublime), sometimes nursing homes or psychiatric hospitals. Then again, it could suggest (depending on one's mood) that "hope springs eternal" or else that there was a "terrible irony" in this impossible pastoral ideal: either way, it struck me as the perfect way to describe the plight of a defenseless virgin left alone on this ravaged earth. Which is to say, all of those institutions might have been called the same thing, and my very literary attraction to this one name was a cover-up, since this disabled little girl could have been taken to any number of places without her having any more say in the matter than anyone did when it came to school. Because for reasons that were beyond me but which, to my bitter, rather churlish mind, made an intuitive sense, the area was swarming with such centers, classed by the kinds of disability they treated, or openly failed to treat: Brignat, Le Reray, La Bouchatte, and that was only to name a few. I had some firsthand experience of these places because I'd played soccer against a few of them with the local police club, whose barracks were stationed nearby; these were *handicapped* matches where we faced opponents not only incapable of grasping the simple rules of the game, but, what's more, who were seized by panic and ran all over the place like decapitated chickens, screaming with fright when the ball came their way, scoring almost half the fifteen to twenty goals we racked up against their team. And because we weren't short of adolescent "team spirit," which sometimes makes "Hitler Youth" seem no more than a tautology, we taunted one of these kids by asking him his name—only to watch him, after a sickening pause, as though already completely lost, stutter his way through the institution's name and *not his own*, a name he'd taken pains to learn by heart and which now teetered on the brink of oblivion. I vividly remembered one of these matches we played against Brignat: a youth worker, one of those Robespierres in dirty tracksuits who for some reason rejoiced in the crude brutality of competitive sport, decided to call an imaginary penalty against us, perhaps to correct the general injustice of the world through one small transgression of his own, possibly as a check against his sporting impulse to eliminate the weak. After endless and confused debate in the opposing team (their shouts billowing from the outlines of their heads like the bright scribbles of children with felt-tip pens), a boy stepped forward to shoot. I'd come across him years earlier when I was in first grade and he was *already* eleven years old (only later did I imagine how humiliated he must have been each time a gang of new boys arrived to start the school term while he sat condemned as though chained to a magic desk that shrank with every passing year, a humiliation he covered up by chewing erasers, a habit he and I, oddly enough, had in common). After moving toward the ball to take the penalty, the boy did not shoot, instead he tried over and over, despite a series of warnings, to *dribble*, head down, into the goal. His persistence may have been funny and exasperating, but his blind rage was also, however stupid, a noble charge against the so-called order of the world; and that attitude I considered MY OWN and identified with wholeheartedly: because my intelligence, carefully crafted to satisfy all the demands of my teachers, right down to the essential touch of originality that would set me apart, was, when you thought about it, nothing more than the way *I* dribbled straight into the goal to score my qualifying penalty. Maybe I found this girl even more touching because I suspected her own weakness held none of the rage and anguish I'd witnessed and embraced at the games—and I would therefore have to find something else to bring us together. On my melancholy trips home from these places that I imagined to be as cursed as the one she returned from, while I sat surrounded by the sounds of normal kids shouting dirty songs, I couldn't help wondering whether, just once, or maybe every day, she felt the same sadness on her way home—probably not, though, because this was *her* natural state—or whether, in a way, I actually expected my own feelings to come back with her on the bus, as though I wanted her sadness to be my own, as though, even with the world against us, we could have our unlikely, longed-for rendezvous, right here at the bus stop, for—or despite—the very reason that everything seemed to separate us, "everything" being a few dismal meters of asphalt road, which looked the same from both sides but which clearly pointed in two opposite directions. But if neither sadness nor rage could unite us, I didn't know what could—the more I wanted to identify with her, the more I identified with myself; and the more I tried to understand her, the less, necessarily, I succeeded: the failure of an intelligent mind to grasp feeblemindedness was deep and dark, no less than the failure of a feeble mind to grasp intelligence, because intelligence got its shape by not understanding the thing it could never be. Since I'd never been a compassionate person and had always considered other people—with the exception of one or two vibrant characters—with suspicion and even disapproval, I had to imagine that my easy empathy for this girl and her spiky hair must apply just as much to a version of my own existence, an idea of what my life would be like if somebody took away, altogether or partly, the mental faculties that let me show off for adults and be rewarded for it (though I'd long ago realized that the kingdom they claimed to rule was nothing but one tiny province in a much bigger empire where they were nothing but pawns: that in dealing with grown-ups you kept coming up against one kind of disability or another, a thing that was disconcerting at first, but more and more reassuring when you realized that the judgments they handed down had no authority). The idea of my own mental deficiency, and my resulting destitution and vulnerability, an idea that was completely absurd and empty seeing as it corresponded exactly to my *blind spot* as an intelligent person, was therefore what filled me with this sorrowful compassion, so unusual for me. Not to say that my interest in this girl, who would always remain a child, implied an indifference to her actual personality, a personality so much more mysterious than the vaunted depths of human psychology. The opposite was true: I couldn't patronize her because, while she might seem to be a young *person*, she was also this *thing* that my so-called intelligence bumped up against when it reached its own limits; an intelligence that, in truth, it would have been less taxing to use in other ways. So the potential advantage I had over her, fully endorsed by a society that had calculated our IQs and sent us in two different directions on two different buses, was, as far as she was concerned, a "dead letter." This was clear from the way she never returned my gaze when I looked at her, so that my own existence, hard enough for me to maintain with any robustness to myself, was, for those dark eyes—black as the inside of closed fists, reflecting less the outside world than the abandoned interior of a skull—a thing she never recognized but saw as a hazy blip on the landscape of those school mornings, an unremarkable little figure standing in front of the already shabby backdrop, a simple outgrowth, barely organic, of the bus shelter I leaned up against, my hands in my pockets, brain blowing on my eyes as though they were embers, trying to make my "passion" seem that much more notable, more incandescent, but failing to send it over to the other side, across the cold magma frozen into tarmac by the organized disaster called society. There were two ways to think of this obvious lack of recognition, and both suited me, for different reasons. The first, in keeping with my low opinions of romantic love, and perfectly appropriate for my age, was that my love, if ever I could make it halfway visible in the too often cold and clammy air that lay between us, would be doomed to a disappointment that matched the intensity of my feelings, in which case my sincerity, underwritten by the pain I'd have to feel, would no longer be in doubt, however unlikely the source of it might be. The second was that this love represented—not despite the lack of acknowledgment but precisely because of it—a blissful reprieve from the war I was waging against the "world," a war that basically depended on getting grown-up approval for what I was good at, and on my belief that I was using this approval to play them, to play them so well, in fact, that it was sometimes hard to tell where the lines of battle were actually drawn. So, now that I could do without all this plotting and scheming, my feelings became "pure"; I could leave the conflict behind and, at the very same time, deliver the final blow. My love, though unspoken and vowed to silence, became a kind of strategic maneuver and stood in danger of losing its spontaneity and, some would say, its value. But at this point the misery I felt at her lack of recognition always came to the rescue and piled itself up like slabs of raw meat on the true balance of my feelings; and anyway, the idea that spontaneous feelings were better than others, well, this struck me as open to debate. I heard a song that nailed it: *"And if the day came when I felt a natural emotion / I'd get such a shock I'd probably lie / in the middle of the street and die."* Where were these so-called natural emotions and why were they worth more than the others? Hadn't I already begun to suspect that with feelings, as with revolutions, the more spontaneous-seeming were actually the outcome of long and involved tactical maneuvers? And if, unfortunately, you had to make do without being "natural," wasn't it better to act as consciously, as deliberately, and therefore as forcefully as possible? Just because a feeling had been painstakingly pieced together didn't mean it was worthless, nor was it necessarily shallow; as far as I could see from the time I'd spent in school playgrounds, or at parties, leaning up all night against the kitchen sink, glancing anxiously around the room, a smile plastered to my face like a dirty Band-Aid that had come half unstuck and that must soon be torn off in pain, this teenage "living in the moment" was in fact secondhand—it had been taught, and by teachers who as role models left much to be desired. These feelings of adolescent immediacy, swimming around in a haze of half-formed emotions, were all just smudged copies of originals that were artificial in the first place, so that they started to look deformed and repulsive, like the muddled organs of a human embryo: no doubt a few years down the line fatal memories of those love affairs would come back to us—well, to *them*, at least—with shudders of embarrassment. So in some ways what I was doing here, at the mercy of the inhuman school bell, freezing and waiting, was just a more radical and ambitious version of what everyone else was doing, except that my feelings, considering how carefully I'd refined them, were at least as close to me as my flesh, and the fact that this was a solitary effort gave it not just the legitimacy of blindness—mine voluntary, hers unavoidable—but also "the elegance of a mathematical formula," to use that baffling expression favored by all the math teachers I'd ever come across, each of them notably lacking in elegance. Yes, my feelings might have corresponded with the pathetic, self-important claim that inexperienced lovers can "love enough for two," but the tyrannical mawkishness of that idea (an idea I knew all about) had nothing to do with what was going on, since my own feelings could never be a burden, because *for her* they'd simply never exist, any more than lots of even more obvious things, for her, would simply never exist—the same way the elegance of a mathematical formula didn't exist for me. I had to admit that this lack of recognition was the basis of all my grand elaborations. The great passion I meant to have was, to be honest, a sort of cliché raised to a higher power, but at least this once I had chosen the cliché for myself. There was no getting around the fact that I hardly ever "went out" with girls, and if I had to name a disability in myself to account for this I had no further to look than my pathological failure to meet the standards of adolescents my age. When I considered their typical range of interests (the rock bands scribbled in felt-tip pen on their shapeless bags were almost always at the top of the charts, and invariably also the crappiest), it was easy to turn my deficiency into a source of proud disdain: but even then there were always traces—some easily erased, some stubborn—of despair. There was more than one explanation for my lack of popularity, all of them roughly along the same lines: for instance, despite living on the outskirts of town, if the middle of nowhere has any outskirts, I didn't have a scooter, much less a car, sexual prostheses without which, in a town like Montpérilleux, I was irrevocably condemned to a cringing and miserable love life. But the biggest problem I faced was my tendency, from very early on and anytime I could, to take things much too seriously, given my hostile surroundings and, above all, my sorry lack of *dignity*, one of the more charming features of macho adolescent males. So I could see that, where feelings were concerned, I too was slightly deficient, and that my latest romantic escapade merely rehashed the old drama of "feelings too deep for words," except this time nobody cared and no one would find out and no one would ever make fun of me. For if this young retarded girl stood as a reflection of my own failure to fit in, when I gazed narcissistically into the slimming mirror of my own weakness, her image also kept this weakness, for once, safely from view. Never in all this had it occurred to me that a certified retard would be easier to seduce than a girl at school, and if I had thought of it, and followed this train of thought to its logical conclusion, and contemplated the likely outcome—boundless admiration, total appreciation, infinite gratitude, the fawning love of a dog for its master—it would have been only for a second, as a vague possibility I dismissed with a nervous laugh. If I'd ventured any farther down this cynical, twisted path than was necessary in order to simply and loyally exhaust all the possibilities, that would have meant I'd hit rock bottom, that I was a real sexual *desperado*; while, on the contrary, I was proud of my hopeless love, and I wanted to cultivate it and use it as a secret weapon, I wanted to sweep the world with a dazzling laser beam of insight. This young girl, this dark-haired child, as far as I could tell from a few meters—a *good* few meters—away, had another clear advantage: she gave me no reason to renounce a particular look I was so partial to. Judging from where I stood, I saw no sign on her little face—of the smeary stigmata of idiocy, no traces of the printless thumb that might have blotted her features like clay, leaving behind areas of whitened flesh like uncharted lands on an old planisphere. Her face—pierced with two black holes as though two fingers had punched through a paper mask—struck me, rather, as *attuned*, with a sort of swiftness—as though it were always coming to the point—that I sought in every face I loved: a veiled landscape of simultaneous upheavals linked by a secret, ever-shifting convergence. Except in her the swiftness produced a kind of excess and disorder: when you peered hardest into her face, what made it so active was really the breakdown of synchronization between its different parts, now in motion, now immobile, but never according to the pathway or sequence you would expect—so that, by these skips, delays, gaps, contradictions, each feeling, real or mimicked, seemed instead to cause a state of general agitation, an uncontrollable panic, like small white mice scattering over a floor.

Oddly, though, this only made her face more lively—she seemed really to *face* the world, and her gaze came at me as if by catapult. The eyes darted first, madly. The pallor that surrounded them seemed even fresher, even whiter, now that it had been left behind: reluctantly it came trailing like a sheet flapping in the wind. I loved the way her features came unstuck, though I couldn't account for it. Maybe her beauty was trying to get out, afraid of lying useless, captive, misunderstood. Such was the explanation I drew from a story that weighed within me with the slight but irksome pressure of a lead bullet they couldn't remove, a story about a very, very beautiful young girl in the tenth grade who, one Saturday evening, in *the* neighborhood disco, the Manoir (naturally, the only time I was allowed to go was when it was a zoo and I was taken there to watch a little menagerie of guinea pigs and hamsters running circles in their cages or going nowhere on their wheels—and had it ever really changed?), had, by due democratic and drunken process, been elected Miss Manoir. The event was celebrated with the bottomless abandon of Saturday nights in Nowheresville, so much so that a gang of "buddies" had to *carry* and *seat* their friend at the steering wheel of the car in which he would drive her home—fast (there, you see, she was among those teenagers so beautiful that their boyfriends own cars rather than scooters or bicycles). Once the car had turned into a pumpkin smashed up against a tree, Miss Manoir never emerged from it again, except in a wheelchair, where she would remain forever after. Her image sat enthroned somewhere in me, young beauty condemned to the wheel, a pretty face posing for an unseen, sadistic painter, her looks withering where she sat, her beauty a ghost far from its manor, drip-fed its vanished past through hour after hour after hour of immobility. Into her paraplegia I read a deplorably sweeping moral concerning all such small-town girls with whom

I might easily enough fall in love—but whom I'd have to flee so as not to see what their futures held in store. My own young love, whose pale face lent itself to those visions of disaster, embodied only too well the doomed flight of beauty from what would kill it, a flight I hoped nevertheless to abet, in my heart, for her sake, unbeknownest to her. Reluctantly I sharpened this bristling little epiphany by summoning up the magic powers of the English word *girl*, as somber and concise as a death rattle in the throat of one strangled by a beloved hand (as opposed to *fille*, which has all the desolate charm of a blond hair left behind on a pillow). I couldn't help but notice that she was as thin as could be, that her jeans, meant for seven- or eight-year-olds at most, yawned and creased around an intangible absence of buttocks, as though her diminished, two-dimensional form had also been refused the trappings of femininity. Hips or breasts, such as fairies scatter over cradles in haste, without a thought for the consequences, would have been overdecoration on a body like hers, would have introduced to the equation of her and me—insoluble, of course, but at least I would find the right words to express it—that x which froze the word *sex* in a sudden grimace of perplexed disgust. The lack of this *common ground* spared me the very worst pangs of jealousy, which I'd always felt was the underside of beauty, like a lining that catches and tears. If she'd been *shapely*, those shapes would slowly have opened her up to the outside world, would have opened a shell that I wanted to keep fragile and closed, and her attractiveness, added to her vulnerability, would no doubt have drawn in probing fingers and untoward, irreparable caresses whose degree of premeditation was, to my mind, irrelevant, innocence and vice being equals in savagery. Maybe she would even have found that the predatory swellings that had taken over her body drew the kind of attention that, before, she'd been granted only because of what she lacked, and she might have felt, in a dark corner of her surprised consciousness, something click into place, the birth of a new kind of power, a premature self-confidence bound to end in disaster. I could only sigh with relief that things were otherwise with her, not only because, as I said, I would have been jealous of other lovers, but also because I was spared from contemplating any possible urges of my own. Not that I generally had any qualms at the thought, arising more from the shallow excitement of belonging than from any deeply felt desire, of groping the first breast that came my way (and all the same, how strangely *real* it felt, and what an amazing renewal of that inexhaustible strangeness, whenever it actually happened) during the feeble saturnalias of afternoons at the pool, or on foreign exchange programs. But—slightly retarded in this respect as well—I was slow to seize the chance when it came along, which showed that maybe, despite myself, I was less of a toad than I might have been. It had never even occurred to me to try this kind of thing out on her, because she was so thin that to imagine her with no clothes on was to reduce her to nothing at all. Or more exactly, even if I had been consumed by this idea with the avid intensity you would expect, it was for all kinds of reasons cut off, more or less, from "reality," and it certainly bore no relation to the questionable levels of reality I was maintaining under the flimsy roof of the bus shelter every morning. Maybe it was from reading too much, or seeing too many forbidden movies, or from the gloomy music in which I steeped my aching hormones—*Pornography* was the cruelest example—I'd prematurely hit on the ragged idea, stitched together as best I could, that sex was deeply connected to corruption, of both body and spirit, and that it violently held all the truth that should ever matter to any human being worthy of the name. But this feeling was accompanied by my tragic tendency, as

I've already mentioned, to be too sentimental—
so that I experienced two feelings at once, albeit
as separate and fiercely indifferent to each other
as two little cars speeding along an electric track.
There was a time when I'd gone off the rails
myself, carving a ludicrous nickname on my forearm with a box cutter, reconciling, in the short
space of time my wound took to heal, my taste
for rose water and my taste for blood—you could
call it my beginnings as a writer. That episode
aside—and there was nothing very sexual about
it anyway—"sex" and "feelings" seemed to belong to completely different *realms*, like the basic incompatibility of two organs which, if they
could be grafted together, would produce no
more than horrific disappointment. So the special
kind of love I'd decided to feel for this young girl
had nothing to do with sexual victory. I knew
that sex was out of the question (at least where I
was concerned, although, as I said, I might doubt
other people's intentions), and this certainty

probably had something to do with a little girl who'd lived in the neighborhood our placid petit bourgeois family had just moved into, oblivious to the trap that was closing in on us, installing ourselves in our "Phoenix Houses"—a strange choice of name, given that it conjured up, with reckless optimism, a pyromaniac's matchstick. One day, I was playing by a stream on a little patch of green bordered by sickly trees when this girl—she was about seven years old and I was ten or eleven—came to join me. I remember the grass, sharp and shiny with rain, the rust of dead leaves, my red-and-green tracksuit, and, even more mortifying, the rubber boots I was wearing. I also remember the shock and surprise I felt when her cold, limp hand pushed away my trouser elastic and grabbed hold of my penis, which shriveled itself into an impossible shell. And yes, maybe I was sexually awakened, but if so, I was like a rigid Playmobil figure, with its unsettling stare and useless, prehensile hands.

While this was unfolding, something in me knew I was *lucky*, as though a muddled half-formed dream of mine had come to fulfillment, and that this was a wonderful opportunity, and might never come my way again—but, at the same time I froze, suddenly, instinctively certain that there was *no way* her hand should stay in my pants for another second. I suppose I may have been afraid that her parents, or mine, would find out about this little scene and fail to appreciate its pastoral charms, but I also felt, just as clearly—and this was a feeling, not an idea, because the idea told me exactly the opposite—that there was something *horrifying* about what she was doing, something only just dawning on me, a still-hazy feeling which, however, I came to understand when I later discovered that her tiny, audacious hand had made its way into my pants not because I was endowed with any particular charm—that was a long way off yet—but because she'd been taught a sinister lesson by our neighbor, a sporty-looking man who drove a BMW, knocked his wife around when he was drunk, and who "played doctor" with his kids. She hadn't been preyed upon, as the rest of us nearly were, by the old wreck who prowled the neighborhood in his rattling car, leaning across to offer us a ride home, but instead, by the terrible childishness of her own father. And when I contemplated my new love, I wanted to bear this lesson in mind: my own excesses frightened me less than those I might discover in her—the filthy traces of other awful people, made worse by her clumsy attempts to mimic the things they'd done that would make this worse still—and none of it, worst of all, would have anything to do with me. Her chastity, to the negligible degree that it was under my control, suited me well since, instead of the complex chaos of action, I preferred the varied, more branching pathways of my dreams. I would much rather summon up an imaginary future in which the bus, as a reward for my patience, would bring me my love, fresh, beautiful, all bundled up in her anorak, and the moment it got to those traffic lights at the crossroads over there, the ones that in my memories are always unwaveringly red, I would know that, despite living in a world where, let's face it, nothing unexpected ever happened, it had been worth the wait. And during those endless suburban seconds that stood between me and her morning pickup, I liked instead to imagine the veiled, gray light of dusk, under the flowering mauve shadows cast by melancholy streetlamps, when her little matchstick form would be surrendered to me, and she would move forward as though forced to walk a tightrope, so thin it was hard to tell whether she was slender or gaunt (like those painfully young gymnasts or ice-skaters whose so-called feminine grace, pared to the bone, is transformed into a fine translucent film of anorexic pallor shimmering over the *danse macabre* of their routines); her spiky hair reminding me of Struwwelpeter's (I'd come across the book in the bedroom of a little girl, the daughter of family friends, and discovered its cruel illustrations, the sinister Gothic lettering, stories twisted and sadistic and therefore perfect for those hasty, fumbling erotic games children like to play on the other side of bedroom walls behind which they hear the grown-ups talk and laugh, mouths full of salted peanuts), hair that made her look like a little mad scientist who thought she'd uncovered the formula for eternal youth in the bottom of her test tube and had suddenly found herself, ruffled by the force of the explosion, standing in the wreckage of her laboratory; or, then again, maybe her hair was standing on end because of an idea she'd just had, or was just about to have, that hadn't yet found its way into words, and maybe it was an idea so brilliant that it must remain forever suspended in the shock of discovery, frozen in this astonished state since words were too small to contain what was vast and unknown, her face, the face of a genius, both uncomprehending and enraptured, caught in the moment of ravished stupidity that marks the pinnacle of intelligence. And when she came back, her mother would be waiting to take her hand, or so I imagined, standing there like an extra in a play, the oblivious witness to our impossible love. Or maybe her mother would be slightly late, for which I'd thank her inwardly, since that would spare me from having to spend too long in her useless presence, unless I was in a good mood and later came to regret not having looked her right in the face as I would have done any other grown-up. This delay might be a matter of ten seconds, in any case, as if to draw notice, in the midst of her admirable punctuality, to the daily sacrifices it took to be on time, as if to let people know how hard it was to meet the bus and collect a child who was not quite right, to show the same old excitement at being reunited with her, as though she were alert, as though she were normal and could just as easily have walked home by herself. It occurred to me that by being meticulously on time, her mother was showing the world that she rejected her daughter's developmental "delay," a word that took on a magical aura, given the thoughts it set in motion: what it meant to be delayed (there was no mistaking the word's connotation—*despite oneself*) as opposed to arrested (which seemed more ambiguous). There was something alluring about the equivocal word *delayed*, like the jittery excitement you might feel when you strayed, even just a little, on your way to school, roaming over some muddy building site along a bulldozer's tracks, the secretly scornful pleasure of letting yourself be overtaken by damp and smoking specters when you were made to run around one of those stadiums in the cold drizzle of a late autumn morning, but also, at the same time, feeling as if it were burrowing into your belly, the imminent punch in the gut, the fear of one whose delay will be punished, the fear of not being able to keep up with the others whose pace you will never match. (I know the feeling so well: oh, those drills, those so-called field days, white T-shirts and navy shorts, the group gymnastic demonstrations in front of the rusting bleachers, the petty, crumbling show of republican power.) In English sometimes they call a mentally disabled person a *retard*, and there is a kind of accidental poetry in naming a human being with this quality of latency or absence, like a clock left behind in an empty room, a page someone forgot to rip out of a calendar, the walking embodiment of jet lag. That was how I felt about myself, notwithstanding the ways in which, according to all those paid experts, I was "ahead." In asking myself these questions, idle themselves, and conceived as a kind of inner delay, as so many minutes stolen from the world, I understood the behavior of Jean-François, the neighborhood idiot, in a new way. He was officially about ten years older than me, although in truth his age had nothing much

to do with real dates and hovered between childhood and the already wrinkled face of someone
in his forties. When we dawdled on the road,
between rows of houses, each just like the other,
homes I liked to picture abandoned one day by
grown-ups so we could take them over with our
restless games, he'd come running toward us, full
of warmth and affection the girls and their
mothers met with uncertain smiles. He'd grab
your wrist and hold it too hard, stammering his
way through his ritual sentence, ultimately recognizable as "Let me see your watch." But he'd
already helped himself to it anyway, and scruti-
nized it for a long time, from up close, his eyes
fizzing with myopic delight, then press his ear
against the mechanism for seconds that sometimes seemed to stretch beyond those ticking by
on the watch's second hand while, *all this time*, he
sniggered with pleasure, dumbstruck. He considered each and every second as if he'd never
encountered one before, as if the time it kept was

a permanent surprise. Looking back on these little performances, I thought one might chalk them up to a dim awareness that other people and even his own body accused him of lagging behind, to a wish he might feel to see himself accurately reflected just once in time's mirror— although the worry I liked to imagine he felt was probably, for him, not much more than a foggy presentiment, and it was more likely that what caused this relentless enthusiasm was a simple pleasure he took in time itself, albeit the petty, mechanical timekeeping of a watch: a perfect synchronization, in fact, of a world where there was no delay. (There's a more profoundly obscure version of this allegory, confirmed by witnesses: a young retarded boy asks his teacher if she wants to know the time, and without waiting for her reply he unzips his fly to reveal a watch he has strapped around his penis.) And I wanted to believe that my beloved lived in *this* kind of time: that here, repetition was always miraculously renewed and ultimately unfathomable—and, after all, what could possibly be better suited for love than this kind of eternity? There was another version of this perpetual delay that fascinated me, suggested by a man whose strange, elongated shadow loomed and hovered mysteriously over the world—well, mine at least: Ian Curtis. "The Eternal": that was what he'd called one of the songs from *Closer*, Joy Division's second album, which I'd managed to unearth in another town, not in Montpérilleux, of course, because it was preordained—as if by a kind of plot to make you give up hope—that you wouldn't find anything that lifted a corner of the veil within a hundred kilometers, so I was sure some sort of revelation must be engraved into the vinyl, and I listened to the album intently, again and again, in the hope that I would discover what that was, thinking it might be as vital as the truths stowed away in my precious books, repositories of the secret knowledge that comes to life as the eye travels like a diamond needle over the furrowed grooves of ink on the page. That song, the second-to-last on side two, began with what sounded like the relentless, circular sound of cicadas, which then suddenly shifted into a kind of electronic whirring noise, not unlike the sound the world makes when you block your ears with your fingers then unblock them over and over. A flat, nasal melody wove itself in like a dirge, steadied by the bass, lashed with a muffled snare so taut and resonant that it sounded like a shallow breath, the toms as hollow as an empty stomach, then the sound of a piano, a note here and there, heavy with meaning at first, soon interspersed with others, scattered, distracted, aimless, as though a child were picking out notes with one finger. Even if you were being self-indulgent, as teenagers are, and you were convinced—in your desperate attempts to probe the bloody wound of an essential feeling, a feeling so strong that, inevitably, some part of it would have to be faked—that the piano music was bringing you closer to the heart of the matter, to the mysteries of existence, you also found yourself thinking, without quite daring to admit it, that the phrasing sounded a bit too classical, that it might just be too sentimental, and the very moment you had that thought, you heard a voice settle on you with the barely trembling calm of the hand that will close your eyes forever. At first, the story it told didn't make any sense to me, but I managed to piece some of it together with the help of already dated magazine interviews (my story takes place in an eternal 1984). It's about a retard whose age we don't know, though everyone treats him like the child he no longer is (one line, *"with children my time is so wastefully spent,"* put it horribly and precisely), confined *ad eternam* to a garden in the suburbs, watching a Catholic procession file past, unendingly slow like "clouds in the sky," scattering petals carried away by the rain. Then you understood: it wasn't that the song tried to mimic mental confusion or some species of aphasia, but instead, and this was the source of its power, it gave you the boy's stiff, contorted dignity, his own perspective and his testimony—"*Try to cry out in the heat of the moment / Possessed by a fury that burns from inside*" (there's no point trying to translate it, *il tente de hurler dans la ferveur de l'instant, possédé d'une fureur qui le brûle tout entier*, you might as well try *singing* it in French)—and this was what I found beautiful, this aborted attempt to release something too strong, too unlikely for others to grasp, like that film I saw, late at night, mesmerized by the flickering glare of the television, one of those glorious moments when parents sleep in their rooms and teenagers finally get to master the world from the sofas they sink into (that's the way I would want to see *Flowers for Algernon*, that's the way I should have seen it, when I was much younger, though I didn't; where a retarded man had an operation and suddenly found his genius could outrival the twists and turns of a mouse in a labyrinth before he became stupid again and went back to square one: thus began, for me, one of those fascinations, injected straight to the brain, that seem to guide you as if by instinct to some deep truth), a film, therefore, seen one of those evenings and instantly assigned to the Book of Important Things, *Freaks*, where Lilliputians, Siamese twins, and living torsos found out what entitled them to the simple emotions their mutilated, deformed bodies had denied them— namely, murder. Here, too, I recognized—easily, from firsthand experience, since this kind of thing happened at my age—*the heat of the moment*, the very instant you knew you should be feeling something but, for various reasons, partly due to inexperience, partly to a desynchronized, muddled teenage constitution, this emotion, however hard you tried to express it, stayed uncomfortably stuck in your heart, only half there and only half felt, just like my love for that girl across the street, the feeling I was trying to coax out of myself the way you might squeeze a toothpaste tube you'd decided to roll from the bottom up but that, distracted, and in a rush, you finally ended up pressing any which way. In the song, this half-man whose world was reduced to a wall, a fence, and a gate was furious both at being buried alive in his own skin and at watching the priests *celebrate* God's will as they go to bury somebody else before his very eyes (my aunt, who looked after children with Down syndrome in a religious institution, told me, horrified, that the children were made to kneel every day, clumsily of course, in front of a plaque that exhorted them to "thank the Lord for the kindness He has bestowed upon us." I have a prophecy of my own: that soon the day will come when man shall bitterly repent having neglected, scorned, or renounced his duty to spread, wherever he might, the simple light of unbelief). But the boy himself is the only "Eternal": standing in the garden at dawn, reduced to the secret horror that keeps him from yelling from the depths of the suburban nightmare that imprisons him, condemned to accept, astonished, his slow spiraling descent into decay. *"No words could explain, no actions determine, / Just watching the trees and the leaves as they fall."* The strong feeling of not being able to express any feelings at all reminded me of the mad panic that gripped you when the telephone worked in only one direction and a voice filtered through while no one could hear you; or else it reminded me of the worst kind of throbbing, recurring nightmare, where other people gather around a corpse that you realize is your own, and your thoughts persist, but however hard you try, you can't even move your little finger, release your jaw, or lift an eyelid: you try to shout but no one hears, you force yourself to move but your limbs fail, you have no eyes to cry with—the fear of being buried alive was nothing more than a projection or even a continuation of this dream, and it was surely the closest you could come to knowing what death was like, the *deadest* idea you could have of it. And the little retarded girl across from me, whose own cry I was straining to hear—it was from this death that I hoped, by listening, to save us. But in my very own waking dream, which offered no more shelter than did reality, her mother would grab hold of her child's delay only to disappear with it, and so that morning, the real morning before my imaginary evening, I would have to satisfy my curiosity by nourishing my imagination on nothing more than supposition. If I tried, assuming they always came by foot, to deduce a probable starting point for their morning walk, still the only way home I liked to picture was a certain avenue that would require them, once they had left the bus stop, to go past the gates of the technical school, then follow the long graffitied wall of the barracks, then turn toward a crossroads that revealed the same gray view in each direction. Why this avenue offered itself up to my imagination I never wondered, so eager was I to return to it and bring progressively into view the numbered dots with their occult shape, like one of those puzzles for summer vacations that aggravate to the point of stupor the very laziness they're supposed to allay. (In another version of this kind of puzzle, you had to find your way out of a labyrinth, like the retarded boy in *Flowers for Algernon*; here, too, it was easy to see myself. And "spot the difference" applied to life itself: the world I lived in was a bad copy of the original missing illustration and I was sure I was one of the mistakes you had to spot.) There was a girl at school who lived on this avenue—I could easily have fallen in love with her if I'd wanted—and I'd visited her one day, on a whim, to discover that while she had perfectly normal hearing, her parents were deaf and dumb. I was taken aback by this revelation, because I'd never imagined that normal children could have disabled parents, that it could be the other way around. And I wondered what it must have been

like to live through a silent childhood, interrupted every now and then by the odd gesture,
or strange vocal sounds. People assumed that language was the best way for children and their
parents to communicate with one another, but
there was plenty of evidence to the contrary—a
girl showed up at school one morning with red
streaks on her face, her mother having tried to
scratch her eyes out after a lively *discussion*—and on
top of it, this communication was so praised by
the powers that be that you couldn't help feeling
suspicious: in fact, it might well be riskier to
reveal much of anything to one's parents; bur-
dened as they were by the course of their own
imperfect lives and likely to react to secrets or
confessions with the usual defenses: scornful
dismissal or a panicky, fawning appeal to a ri-
diculous army of experts. Since this young girl
struck me as the less unbalanced of the two of
us, it rather stood to reason that there might be
unexpected advantages to our thwarted means

of communication, it might teach people, for instance, that different generations never could be reconciled, that they were deaf to each other to a degree that no clumsy demagogue could ever heal them: each of us was, by right and by virtue of that beautiful, maligned word *individual*, the one and indivisible republic of a self, the only *homeland* we'd ever have, alone in an echoing world where age and language are barriers as natural as rivers and mountains. Having got over their slight and unspoken disappointment at having "normal" kids who soon would have to go live somewhere else and leave their kingdom under the sea, they no doubt "got along" at my friend's house and understood one another just as well as in any other household, perhaps even better, because they were spared the painful pretense of mutual understanding, which, if it does exist, is by no means a given between people who just happen to belong to the same family. But quite beyond what I wanted it to tell me, her journey through town also intrigued me for an entirely contrary reason, that of its insignificance: not for the obvious insignificance that emanated from those places to the casual observer, but for the way this insignificance might be lifted to a higher, an absolute plane. When I tried to imagine what she might be seeing, tried hopelessly to fill in her perceptions, I found that my impressions shaded into a dream in which fleeting shapes kept breaking down and slipping away, constantly reinventing themselves. Even more precisely, although I'd have been hard pressed to lend this any substance, the way I imagined she saw things reminded me of a black-and-white program on public TV (for there is no hiding it, I was born in a distant era: that of my parents) pretentiously named "The Riddles of the Sphinx." Up against the backdrop of the starlit pyramids and the sphinx, letters of the alphabet began slowly to trace their own contours, revealing their identities as their curves unfurled into recognizable shapes, spelling out a message that, if you hadn't yet fallen into a hypnotic stupor, you would gradually be able to anticipate—although, as a child transfixed by the majesty of those letters writing themselves of their own accord, the message itself was still beyond me. And the world must have been equally mysterious to the girl whose journey home I followed in my thoughts. All those jostling messages on posters, on advertisements, on road signs, on storefronts and signposts would be just as opaque: a motley collection of curves and straight lines separated from one another by wide-open spaces, as though stuck, frozen, suddenly interrupted in the middle of tracing out some sort of revelation. These garish signs and posters crowding her on her way, like a mob at a royal procession, found themselves reduced to mere objects, no different from trees and houses, and it was as if you were scratching off a thick layer of dirt, like so much sea foam carried off by a wholesome breeze one wished might never cease to blow: discounted fake food, garden furniture, school supplies, plastic car accessories, all these things dispersing, evaporating, so finally one might breathe. But all the same, once these phosphenes falling on eyes fatigued with reality had burned away, nothing new appeared: it was as though someone had removed the potted plants from the foreground of the set for an end-of-term pageant to reveal just how amateur and inane the whole thing was. The sky wasn't going to get bigger or wider, the air wasn't going to get purer, it was instead as if all these elements had been silenced and were now melting into the backdrop, absorbed by the hopelessness and ugliness of the neighborhood. This princess, the last in line, left a shimmering wake behind her that revealed not the vision of a universe renewed by the refreshing perspective of ignorance, but instead, an empty, exhausted listlessness, a small bloodless world long drained of life and sick at heart, a desert of gloomy streets, interchangeable suburban houses, ugly cars, mismatched and brightly colored, parked haphazardly in front, a town whose drab contours seemed designed to prop up the glaring white sky of a ruined photograph, as though cut out along the dotted lines of the rooftops, spreading out the same, endless oppressive light into the air, as though veiled by the enclosed space of a never-ending afternoon. This was where I had to give up hope and allow her to disappear, while being so familiar with her predicament that I didn't really want to follow her there anyway. But I still wondered what made my experiences any different from hers, what it was that set us apart, if anything: questions like these came and went, coursing through me like clouds. Did she have any brothers or sisters—I didn't—and if she did, were they disabled, too (which would make her in a way the *only* child, the only sister an only son could want to have, the only sibling worthy of him), and beyond those scrambled genes, did she have a father in the background who was busy or who couldn't bear the separation on the sidewalk her mother endured every day? When her mother and father were suddenly left alone, their daughter entrusted to some sort of institution, what was it like between them: Did they hold back sighs of relief, secretly wishing their time to themselves could last longer, or did they feel a yearning for her half-empty presence, this slender pail of the Danaids into which they poured all their attention, including the attention they had promised each other *before*, and had given up as a luxury? Now they were parents of this rough muddled draft of a child, what sort of love did they feel for each other: Was there between them the shadow of blame or else were they, in the English phrase, *thick as thieves*, united against the injustice for which *they* could never be held responsible (but then who could)? Did they find in the willed stupidity of faith the power not to ask themselves these questions or were they (this was not incompatible) activists in some organization as a way to improve their lives at the same time as their daughter's, though she'd never know the difference—maybe they wanted more money, maybe they went on demonstrations and made their daughter hold up one of those placards or banners with a first-person message she was supposed to deliver but that, in fact, she couldn't understand—and suddenly, there she was in another town, she couldn't believe her eyes, it was unimaginably vast, and she was no longer on the sidewalk like the one she was used to but in the middle of a monstrous boulevard, surrounded by a strange, threatening crowd that at the same time cocooned her in murmurs and moving colors she might have followed to the ends of the earth. Maybe they'd brought a lawsuit, seeking vengeance for a mistake that could never be put right but that must be given a human face, no matter what the cost: a careless or self-important doctor, unfeeling or incompetent, one of those more-or-less human-seeming replicants in charge of pharmaceutical companies—just so long as it wasn't their own faces; so long as it wasn't his when, doomed, he ejaculated, nor hers when she welcomed it, rejoicing that she wasn't *protected*; not hers when the doctor told her—a little too late—that she was the chosen one, nor his, when she told him the news. It wasn't so bad, at first: their little girl's feeble mind (but she was so *pretty*) was camouflaged by the fears, the frailty of infancy. Then things just stayed put: her baffling inability to understand anything; her clumsy, late first steps, which she soon abandoned in favor of swaying from one foot to the other; her awkward imitations of their gestures, waving good-bye by throwing up her arm, as if on a spring, her fingers held rigidly together, or using the wrong movement from an already tiny repertoire, like stiffly using her forearm to scratch her head; the words she heard and, incredulous, let float away on the air, ungrasped, bubbles empty of meaning and quick to burst (her little red tongue was like a sticky wrapper stuck to a lemondrop of silence), the great, vivid emptiness of her eyes in which her parents could see nothing but their own intensified distress; the excruciating slowness of it all was enough to drive anyone mad. They had to readjust all their gestures, ham it up, turn every moment into a pointless pedagogical farce. She understood nothing, she learned nothing, so she just stood there, lively sometimes, joyful even, a groundless joy that brought tears to their eyes, though they wished they could share these moments with *her*: her ecstasy over a leaf, which could last for whole minutes at a time, as though it were the most wonderful thing in the world, as though the precise bifurcations of its veins or the carefree elegance with which it swayed in the breeze was what made her clap her hands together in glee; her disconcerting squawks of delight when she saw a tourist brochure, an advertisement, or a piece of paper picked up off the ground. They couldn't always keep her entertained, so sometimes they sat her in front of the television, which she turned to again and again, the way other girls her age gravitated toward their mirrors. She didn't understand any of it, but she loved it all anyway: news, ads, movies all dissolving into a meaningless, structureless fog. I wanted to comfort myself with the thought that her body or her nervous system would keep coming back to what *moved* her, without anyone knowing why that might be—because of a certain color arrangement, perhaps, or the slightest variation in the way something moved, or some music if suddenly, gleefully she recognized the tune or pitch or orchestral arrangement: a few xylophone notes ringing out here and there like sandman's dust, or the kindly bearlike sounds of the cello, or maybe she'd hear the supple, insidious, merciless sounds of the wolf in that record we all had, *Peter and the Wolf*, and feel scared, maybe because she felt her body being transported by a sudden intensity, a rhythmic acceleration, the unforeseen arrival of a new instrument—the same things that made me respond to the bits of music I liked, which weren't always, in fact never were, very sophisticated, but instead tended to consist of wistful, shameful snatches of music: themes from old TV programs, forgotten films, or children's records. I was ready to bet (but what, with whom?) that nature programs were her favorites, with their familiar rhythms as savagery gave way to serenity, animals peacefully devouring one another in a blue fizz of flies, their carnal embraces, their sighs as they napped in the scanty shade of one or two trees— all the things that brought you back to hunger, to exhaustion, to cruelty, to games, to a life freed from freedom itself. I liked to think that she could, just like me, see in these timeless wild animals an inversion of our own predicament: the deafening white noise of a Sunday when you felt yourself trapped like a fly in dusty acrylic curtains (as a child I used to make myself sick by turning around and around in their nets until I'd wrapped myself into a suffocating, dingy cocoon and they pulled on my hair and threatened to scalp me), those Sundays that slowly spread a hissing headache into your neck and then your skull, as though rolling your eyeballs around between their grubby fingers and nails. It really was a cruel irony that these documentaries tended to be shown on days like these: that as they laid bare the slow progress of prehistoric time, the long afternoon of the ages as they unfolded across the screen, they belittled and humiliated us with the baldness of their appetites, the violence of their satiations, as boredom turned into savagery and suddenly flared into passion. That I saw my own unhappy childhood reflected in this young girl was a theory I could not brush aside, but having no objections to offer, I tried hard to play it down. I didn't like what that word—*childhood*—conjured up, or rather, I didn't like the way most people used it: that presumption of innocence and starry-eyed wonder. The only good thing about childhood is that no one really remembers it, or rather, that's the only thing about it to like: this forgetting. What else could possibly lie beneath that blissful oblivion but shame: a dark knowledge of that terrible badge of weakness, that inescapable servitude (bearable only thanks to the slow revelation that we could inflict cruelty and evil on the weaker kids), a sickening awareness that just about everything there is to understand was beyond us, made even worse by the lies and inaccuracies that adults feel entitled to spread around, deliberately, or because they don't know any better, about themselves or about the nature of reality? And that's not even counting the *sheer terror* that could take hold—the slightest thing could do it, a mask, a dummy—at any moment. I didn't really start to live, quite literally, until I was free, as far as anyone can be, from the spells cast by ignorance and childhood feebleness, until I had understood that, as another song put it, *I was not this world and the world was not me*, and that I had nothing to lose because nothing in it was made to fit me or to please me, until I was allowed, or at least when I was able to glimpse, in the suddenly disentangled threads on the page, in the luminous spell cast by a movie, in the emotional upheaval I felt with the punch of a chorus, some evidence as to what surrounded me, and to reconstruct, haltingly at first, the right way to feel and to talk about what was known as *reality*. So the "innocence" of this childhood gaze, which they praised so mindlessly—or maybe it was a black, self-serving attempt to ensure that the trashy inanities that surrounded us were properly maintained and replenished—I didn't think any kid had really experienced it, let alone enjoyed it, except maybe in retrospect, trawling it for salvage though it was already too late: as far as I was concerned, as a reformed ex-child, a proud one, I don't ever remember feeling that I was looking on a brand-new world with fresh eyes. There were, of course, some things that a small child did perceive for the first time, but given the narrow confines of its tiny mental universe, the blankness of its stunted memory, on the whole, adults or teenagers were better equipped to see more, to be more discerning, and, assuming they had their wits about them, to understand these things for the first time. The notion of this powerful childhood gaze was all the more specious given that adults, in the name of that very spontaneity, subjected children to every sort of rehearsed and prepackaged foolishness so that what children were supposed to see and like was no more than the adults' idea of what they imagined having lost themselves, which was in turn probably no more than other versions of childhood recycled by other adults, this cycle of loss building itself up according to the endless demands of nostalgia, so that the older and more rotten the world became, the more this driveling idiocy prevailed and this idea of innocence took hold. Grown-ups tried to sweeten the pill, but there was no hiding it, children were the most *oppressed* creatures on earth. Just look how they were led day and night to their bus stops, in rain or snow or gale-force winds, their bags excessively weighed down by the cumbersome learning of their teachers, forced to go to school to readjust the freshness of their gaze: they were like nothing more—and this applied to their childhoods as a whole—than a stack of colored bricks that grown-ups piled up then toppled with the back of a hand. They saw the world through the dirty windshield of a car that smelled so strongly of hot, dusty plastic that they wanted to throw up, the seats glued to their thighs so firmly as to flay them if they moved. In such conditions, it was highly unlikely that any of us should perceive anything as it was, unless we stumbled, later and more or less by chance, on the formula for that acid bath which could purge one's vision and allow one to reconstruct, in the slanting autumnal light of the very *last chance*, some glimmer of truth. In all my childhood only one perception ever seemed to me now, in hindsight, as having been, to use that beautiful word, *lucid*: the sense that struck me once at day camp, that the people and places all around me, everything in short, was just an elaborate hoax, made up of actors and sets—I didn't know whether to be more surprised by the scope of the thing (no doubt serving some secret purpose that was, unfortunately, beyond me) or by its low budget (which would explain the bad architecture and the extras' general lack of talent), and even if I understood this wasn't literally true, still it was a striking and conclusive glimpse of the fraudulence that surrounded me. So, yes, I wanted my love for this girl to mirror childhood as I knew it: the vulnerability she embodied, the way it made her dance to their tune, manipulated by all sorts of good intentions, all in good conscience. She was like a belief in childhood to which others had clung too long, and now the lie had finally been exposed and all that remained was to keep up appearances while doing the least possible harm. But really I wasn't sure that a word like *childhood* pertained to her at all, since one has a childhood only to lose it, the same as virginity (for all I knew about that). Of the two, she'd lose her virginity first—I thought this with a kind of painful and ferocious pleasure, with all the intensity that we bring to a "displaced" emotion—but wouldn't really be changed by either loss: for in nothing that she lost would there be any sort of revelation, or any possibility of a new beginning. The shame of it, in any case, wasn't that this sappy childhood was lost to time; instead, the shame was that this infantile irresponsibility was encouraged by teachers to persist, and that, by staying put, it became a kind of delay, the remnants of childhood that made retards of us all. But maybe it was better to speak of an *arrest* rather than a delay, a development interrupted at any given moment, as abrupt as it is secret. Don't we all discover at some stage or another that there are some things we'll never get any better at, even though we have no idea why and hardly ever notice it when it happens, even though we may have enjoyed these things and might not have been lagging behind last time we checked? Learning to draw, for instance, was a familiar catastrophe—all of a sudden, unaware, you just stop getting any better at it, your drawings never progress beyond those of a four-year-old or a six-year-old, you're left behind by those who "can draw," condemned to producing flat, doughy figures on the page, with no sense of perspective to them and (this was what really struck me) no resemblance to the outside world: condemned by your ruined self to a shameful childhood. It was the same for lots of other things you were supposed to get better at, and even though the teachers and the coaches—themselves beyond repair—tried their best, they too were stuck, unable to grasp that we just couldn't understand what they effortlessly understood. Something in each of us was broken beyond repair, the mechanism for drawing a person's face or adding up a sum "even a simple one" or moving easily from one printed word to the next: and that's the way it was, everybody was a Russian doll of preserved abortions, a shelf of deformed embryos floating in formaldehyde and arranged according to age, a children's cemetery with its tiny little graves all lined up in a row, with the freshest waiting empty, a failed party where the lights were being extinguished one by one though dawn was hours away. (I had a whole stack of metaphors like these, all the more useful if you *couldn't* draw a person's face to save your life.) So that this paragon of creation, the thing we called adulthood, was no more than a special series of arrested developments, a variation that was socially useful and even encouraged as better suited to the division of labor than was the idiot math prodigy or the mongoloid who could recite the calendar forward or backward. So while she was waiting there, frail to no end, like a signpost when they've torn off the sign, I saw all these possibilities in her that had become impossible, and I projected onto her fragility the immense waste of talent I was forced to observe every day in my closest friends and suffered a little bit too readily in myself, a waste that filled me with a vengeful bitterness and pride at having salvaged or developed a talent that would allow me to forget, even in the moment of giving up on them, my own irreparable limitations which, as they tightened within me, grew and grew. I wanted to turn this little retarded girl I adored, she who would soon be out of reach if I didn't find the nerve to cross the road, into an allegory (though I didn't know the word) of my own handicaps and my friends', or of early promise thrown to the black pigs of Time. The problem wasn't that we didn't *need no education* (on the contrary, it was obvious how badly needed that was); instead, it was our own guilty complicity which—all the while school snipped the live bodies in its care to a pattern of its own unspoken devising, at no little risk to the bodies themselves—turned rebellion into a hopeless enterprise bound to end all too often in humiliation. That's what accounted for the smell of failure that hovered over town, as persistent and sickeningly familiar as the stench from the dog food factory that the breeze carried in and forgot to carry back. As much as I may have wished to revolt, or grasped that revolt was the only noble course of action, I also saw that underneath its seeming diversity of forms, active or otherwise, lay little more than defeat: *c'était magnifique mais ce n'était pas la guerre*. Not that the few protests I contemplated were ever especially grand, or vivid enough to evoke pathos, except perhaps in their profuse mediocrity. They were all retreats, more or less successful, into a position of weakness where I could easily be overpowered without a fight. Opting out of the system may have been one solution, like a brilliant friend of mine who'd suddenly decided, after a motorbike accident, to give up his social life, as though his head had cleared during his convalescence and he'd suddenly, joyfully, been set free, veering away from people forever, just as he'd skidded euphorically off the road, and he never looked back. His sudden withdrawal set in motion little armies of social workers, determined to turn us—his "friends"—into accomplices and spies charged with bringing him back to his senses, which he'd abandoned with no explanation and with no regrets, as though he'd grown sick of all of them all at once. We knocked on his apartment door, but in vain, because all we heard was the straining and panting of his dog behind it, and the murmurs of his voice as he tried to prevent the animal, at least, from betraying him. The rest of the story, which I got second- or thirdhand, involved the various attempts to rescue this intelligence so determined to reject everything around it: endless rehabilitations and training courses that, judging by the rate at which he dropped out of them, made everything worse; he'd last a month at first, then a week, and then, finally, only a day. I had no idea what would become of him, but I knew in the pit of my stomach that he'd thrown away all the beauty and sweetness, all the life in him, and trapped himself in the very ugliness he thought he'd left behind. Another strategy was the slow, dull drift into ready-made forms of delinquency: a little boy, well-groomed, good in math, would all of a sudden, with the help of lots of buttons and clumsily sewn patches, turn into the punk of his neighborhood, coming up with not-very-likely schemes for robbery and dealing pot, forcing himself at every moment to bend, with systematic determination at first, then automatically so as to match the crude caricatures that, if they told the basic truth about "the system" at all (the truth came shooting from the stinking maw of 1977, that much I knew), still told only part of the story, since the system didn't consider it a crime to turn its staunchest self-styled enemies into self-destructive buffoons who'd end up hurting only themselves. And while a loud, badly played guitar, and the insults hurled around so convincingly they seemed to turn in on themselves, might be something I considered heroic, a worthy cause, and if I wanted to expose myself, like the others, to its radiation, it was also, I realized one evening as I pogoed around with thirty other well-behaved people at the only punk show to have lost its way and found itself in Montpérilleux and suddenly understood the singer was *disillusioned* when one fleeting gesture he made betrayed him, nothing more than a nostalgic *no future*, a folklore that, in the final analysis, was obsolete, a wistful strain of night music as sad as wooden chimes playing lullabies above a cradle when you pull a piece of string to start the melody and it slowly winds itself back up while music plays and the child below watches it retreat with the terrible knowledge that silence is on its way. There was a third strategy, which a friend of mine had turned to when he systematically cultivated the kind of eccentricity from which there could be no turning back. This boy, whose bedroom I'd seen full of teetering piles of books topped by the works of Kafka like a prophetic crown, capable of riding his scooter two hundred kilometers there and back to see *Boy Meets Girl* and known for making strange films in which copies of *Das Kapital* grew on trees, had resolved with his pitiless chip-toothed smile, whether at school or on our "main street," to throw himself into all kinds of car accidents, to go around in drag, in general to provoke one catastrophe after another, all of which conferred upon him the status of a madman, and although I couldn't help admiring the *sacrifice* involved, it astonished me that this was a status to which a person might actually aspire. In the end, all these remedies were useless, and maybe they even prolonged the blight we were all subjected to by being born here, in this time and place. Personally, I'd acquired a different kind of itch, having prematurely been encouraged to show off as a child, and having discovered that the capital letter in *Art* was a rocket that could escape gravity and launch me into another orbit, or at the very least to the first floor of the Eiffel Tower, a permanently incomplete version of it, or a half-destroyed one, but from where the sight of the surrounding ugliness would be refreshed. It was very obvious, once I started to listen in the dead of merciful night to a handful of edgy, already outdated songs that sifted through polluted wastelands and the bored ruins of fading industrial towns, that I needed a rock group of my own, so I became the only member of a band I named Proletkult: the only thing it did, against a thin pasteboard background of electronic drumbeats, was mix a little white noise with electric pulses, with the beautiful low-frequency sounds of a synthesizer in which you could distinctly hear electrons bouncing against some sort of sensitive plate like hail. In this sound, too, I wanted to hear a radical protest, rebelling against our plasticized impoverishment, against the grimy cellophane that suffocated us all, although there was certainly nothing more, in the tinny synthetic music of those years, than the sound of impoverishment itself. Maybe making myself hear that noise in my head, maybe setting it down amplified onto noisy cassettes was just my own utterly unoriginal rehearsal, in a minor key, of those teenage suicides, the ones you'd sometimes hear about on those awful school buses with orange leatherette seats, the kind I was waiting for, teenagers who had once too often brandished in a trembling hand their suppressed rage and violence and the war they believed everyone waged against them before they turned that hand against themselves: the crazy little army of teenage suicides, girls and boys with purple lips and wrists wide open, who I dreamed would take up arms and flood our streets like a pale rebellion of indignant ghosts. I dismissed this course of action, sensing my own reserves of strengths, but I experimented with the idea and took it as far as I could in a game I christened Bus Stop: on summer nights, I would stretch out on the road in front of my house, on hot, grainy asphalt scattered with sharp bits of gravel, and watch and wait for growling motors, the blinding movement of headlights, and I weighed up the pros and cons, what tied me to life like a blood oath, what left me cold, or tired me out; and when the noise grew sharper, more grating, and when the headlights from the first bend in the road began to cut out the sides of the buildings and project a slow, revolving shadow dance on the wall, I always came back to the same conclusion—that I felt something stir inside me, as hazy and phony as a childhood memory, as insistent as a hit song you'd heard so often you couldn't get its bitterness out of your head, something that promised me a better future, only somewhere else. And I would unpeel myself from the road, I'd pick myself up, what was left of me, what could still be of some use, and slowly make my way back to the pink gravel of the sidewalk, just like the one my little retarded friend was standing on that morning as stoic as an abandoned house awaiting demolition. Standing there, her silence and her silhouette seemed to send out the cheap synthetic sound of the times, or at least that's what I thought I could hear; one of those falsely upbeat tunes that vibrate from plastic radios, *amoureux solitaires dans une ville morte, amoureux imaginaires après tout qu'importe.* She was like a statue that embodied universal carnage and, at the same time, was unconcerned with the effects of that carnage; she came to represent heedlessness itself—in her, heedlessness had reached its heights of perfect oblivion. She was the living effigy of everything we will never be and, in every sense of the word, she was the retard that I was and that I wasn't, she was my vanishing, wasted talent, and I was the price society paid so that I could become what she couldn't. And this was exactly what I was trying to love; what this little girl, this girl of wire, made it known she could never be: everything that had been, or that would be, no matter who we were, borne away from each of us. And now a big white thing with big clumsy wheels was coming around the bend, its face placid, impassive with huge empty eyes, a savage jaw barely muzzled by the radiator grille. The bus stopped and hid me from my nameless love; it heaved a stinking, weary sigh, swished open its doors with the dry click of metal that belied their whispered invitation. Children's heads bobbed in the misty windows, and among them I thought I could spot her own. It was she, it had to be, who sat there: a little cloud of steam grew bit by bit on the windowpane until it had the contours of a face, and no palm would ever wipe it clear with a wave that I'd have wished so badly to take as a greeting, a wave that I'd have re-turned with a wave of my own, which I alone would have known was a farewell.